Mr. Putter & Tabby
Walk the Dog

CYNTHIA RYLANT

Mr. Putter & Tabby
Walk the Dog

Illustrated by

ARTHUR HOWARD

Harcourt, Inc.
Orlando Austin New York San Diego London

For Herb and Mary
—C. R.

For Cora and Bernie
—A. H.

Text copyright © 1994 by Cynthia Rylant
Illustrations copyright © 2008, 1994 by Arthur Howard

For information about permission to reproduce
selections from this book, please write Permissions,
Houghton Mifflin Harcourt Publishing Company 215 Park
Avenue South NY NY 10003.

www.hmhco.com

First Harcourt paperback edition 1994

Library of Congress Cataloging-in-Publication Data
Rylant, Cynthia.
Mr. Putter & Tabby walk the dog/Cynthia Rylant;
illustrated by Arthur Howard.
p. cm.
Summary: When their neighbor Mrs. Teaberry hurts her foot,
Mr. Putter and his cat, Tabby, agree to walk her dog for a week.
[1. Dogs—Fiction. 2. Cats—Fiction. 3. Old age—Fiction.]
I. Howard, Arthur, ill. II. Title. III. Mr. Putter and Tabby
walk the dog.
PZ7.R982Mv 1994
[E]—dc20 93-21467
ISBN 978-0-15-256259-5
ISBN 978-0-15-200891-8 (pb)

Printed in China

SCP 18 17 16 15
4500484767

1
The Lollypup

Mr. Putter and his fine cat, Tabby,
lived next door to
Mrs. Teaberry and her small dog, Zeke.

Mrs. Teaberry sometimes gave
Mr. Putter eggplant for his supper.
And Mr. Putter sometimes gave
Mrs. Teaberry kiwis for her lunch.

They were very happy
living side by side.

One day Mrs. Teaberry slipped
on a kiwi and hurt her foot.
Mr. Putter and Tabby took her
to the doctor.

The doctor said, "This foot needs a rest.
No walking Zeke for a week."
"No walking Zeke for a week?"
cried Mrs. Teaberry.

"But who will walk my little lollypup?"
(She always called Zeke her little lollypup.)

Then Mr. Putter, who had a
very soft heart, said, "I will.
I will walk your little lollypup."
Mrs. Teaberry was happy.

But she was a little worried.

"I hope he doesn't tug," she said.

"Oh, no," said Mr. Putter.

"Zeke won't tug."

"I hope he doesn't wrap around trees,"
she said.

"Oh, no," said Mr. Putter again.

"Zeke won't wrap."

"And I hope he doesn't chase other dogs," she said finally. "Especially the big ones."

"Oh, no," said Mr. Putter for the last time. "Zeke is a good dog."

"Zeke is a fine dog."

Mr. Putter looked at the little lollypup.

"Zeke is a *dream* dog," Mr. Putter said
with a smile.

2

The Nightmare

Zeke was a *nightmare*.

The first day Mr. Putter and Tabby
took him for a walk, he tugged.

He tugged and tugged and tugged.

He tugged Mr. Putter and Tabby

through yards

and creeks

and houses

they had never been through before.

When Mr. Putter and Tabby got home,
they had to have some warm milk
and pudding
and a nap.

"Zeke is not a dream dog,"
Mr. Putter said to Tabby
when they woke up.
"Zeke is a nightmare."

The second day they
took him for a walk,
Zeke wrapped around trees.
He wrapped around
an elm tree.

He wrapped
around a pine tree.

He wrapped
around a pear tree.

And he always wrapped
Mr. Putter and Tabby with him.

When Mr. Putter and Tabby got home,
they had to have some warm milk
and popovers
and a nap.

"Zeke is not a dream dog,"
Mr. Putter said to Tabby
when they woke up.
"Zeke is a nightmare."

The third day Zeke chased dogs.

And he didn't chase little ones.

He chased big ones.

He chased a Russian Wolfhound.

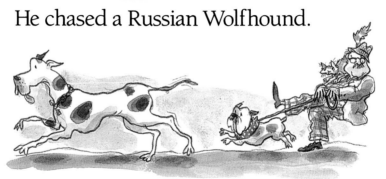

He chased a Great Dane.

He chased a Saint Bernard.

He chased them until they got bored
with being chased.

Then they turned around and chased Zeke.

And Mr. Putter.

And Tabby.

The big dogs chased them
through yards
and creeks

and houses

they had never been through before.

When Mr. Putter and Tabby got home,
they had to have some warm milk
and shortbread
and a nap.
"Zeke is not a dream dog,"
Mr. Putter said to Tabby
when they woke up.
"Zeke is a nightmare."

And the two of them
sat a long time
wondering what to do.
They weren't sure they
could live through
four more days with
the lollypup.

3

The Dream Dog

"Here's the deal, Zeke,"
Mr. Putter said on the fourth day.

"You be a good dog,
and every day after our walk
you'll get a nice surprise."

Zeke was a smart dog.

He knew what a deal was.

The fourth day
he didn't tug,
he didn't wrap,
and he didn't chase.
He was a dream dog.

So Mr. Putter and Tabby took him
to the Frosty Freeze.
Zeke had a hot fudge sundae
with extra cherries.

The fifth day
Zeke didn't tug,
and he didn't wrap,
and he didn't chase.
He was a dream dog again.

So Mr. Putter and Tabby
took him to the swimming pool.
He jumped off the diving board
fifteen times.

On the sixth day
Zeke was a dream dog,
and he went to the carnival.

On the seventh day
Zeke was a dream dog,
and he went to the zoo.

When Mr. Putter and Tabby
took Zeke home for the
last time, Mrs. Teaberry asked,
"Was Zeke a good lollypup?"

And Mr. Putter
(who had brought her pecans
instead of kiwis)
smiled the biggest smile.
He said, "Zeke was a dream lollypup."

Then he and Tabby said good-bye
and went home
and had a party.

The illustrations in this book were done in pencil, watercolor,
gouache, and Sennelier pastels on 90-pound vellum paper.
The display type was set in Minya Nouvelle, Agenda, and Artcraft.
The text type was set in Berkeley Old Style Book.
Color separations by Bright Arts, Ltd., Singapore
Printed and bound by RR Donnelley. China
Production supervision by Christine Witnik
Series cover design by Kristine Brogno and Michele Wetherbee
Cover design by Brad Barrett
Designed by Arthur Howard and Trina Stahl